MW01093553

The Poorest Shepherd

A Christmas Legend

Maura Roan McKeegan

Illustrated by Gina Capaldi

Huntington, Indiana

Dedication

For Jeanne, Teresa, Michele, David, Carole, Catherine, and Anne.
— Maura Roan McKeegan

To my students at Immaculate Conception STEM Academy in Monrovia, California. Each of you brings me so much joy!
— Gina Capaldi

Every reasonable effort has been made to determine copyright holders of excerpted materials and to secure permissions as needed. If any copyrighted materials have been inadvertently used in this work without proper credit being given in one form or another, please notify Our Sunday Visitor in writing so that future printings of this work may be corrected accordingly.

Copyright © 2022 by Maura Roan McKeegan

27 26 25 24 23 22   1 2 3 4 5 6 7 8 9

All rights reserved. With the exception of short excerpts for critical reviews, no part of this work may be reproduced or transmitted in any form or by any means whatsoever without permission from the publisher. For more information, visit: www.osv.com/permissions.

Our Sunday Visitor Publishing Division
Our Sunday Visitor, Inc.
200 Noll Plaza
Huntington, IN 46750
1-800-348-2440

ISBN: 978-1-68192-964-4 (Inventory No. T2694)

1. JUVENILE FICTION—Holidays & Celebrations—Christmas & Advent.
2. JUVENILE FICTION—Religious—Christian—Holidays & Celebrations.
3. RELIGION—Christianity— Catholic.

LCCN: 2022932971

Cover and interior design: Lindsey Riesen
Cover and interior art: Gina Capaldi

PRINTED IN THE UNITED STATES OF AMERICA

Author's Note

From the moment I first heard it, the legend of the poorest shepherd captured my heart.

Variations of this tale have been told in different countries and in different languages. When stories are handed down orally, they often change from one generation to the next, and from one culture to another. Each unique version represents the storyteller's own imagination, experience, and style.

The version in this book reflects the way this story came to life in my imagination. I have retold it here with loving gratitude for the storytelling tradition that preserved this legend.

—Maura Roan McKeegan

In quiet fields,
Where stars shone bright,
Five shepherds watched
Their flocks one night.

David, the oldest,
Fended off sleep
By carving a slingshot
While guarding the sheep.

Caleb, his brother,
Got ready to eat
A cake made with honey
He'd brought as a treat.

Jacob, their cousin,
Pulled his cloak tight.
He was glad for its warmth
On this cold winter night.

Jesse, their neighbor,
Leaned on his crook
As he bent for a drink
From a babbling brook.

Micah, the youngest,
Was hungry and cold,
But he tried to be brave,
And he tried to be bold.

Then all of a sudden,
In front of their eyes,
An angel from heaven
Appeared in the sky.

"Be not afraid,"
He proclaimed to the boys,
For he brought them good news
Of a very great joy!

For to them on that day,
A savior was born
In the city of David:
It was Christ the Lord.

A whole host of angels
Appeared with him then,
Saying, "Glory to God …
And peace among men."

When the angels had left them,
The shepherds made haste
To go see the Infant
And find His birthplace.

And when they arrived
And beheld His sweet face,
They fell to their knees,
Overwhelmed by God's grace.

Mary and Joseph
Watched closely and smiled
As thc shcpherds adored
The divine newborn Child.

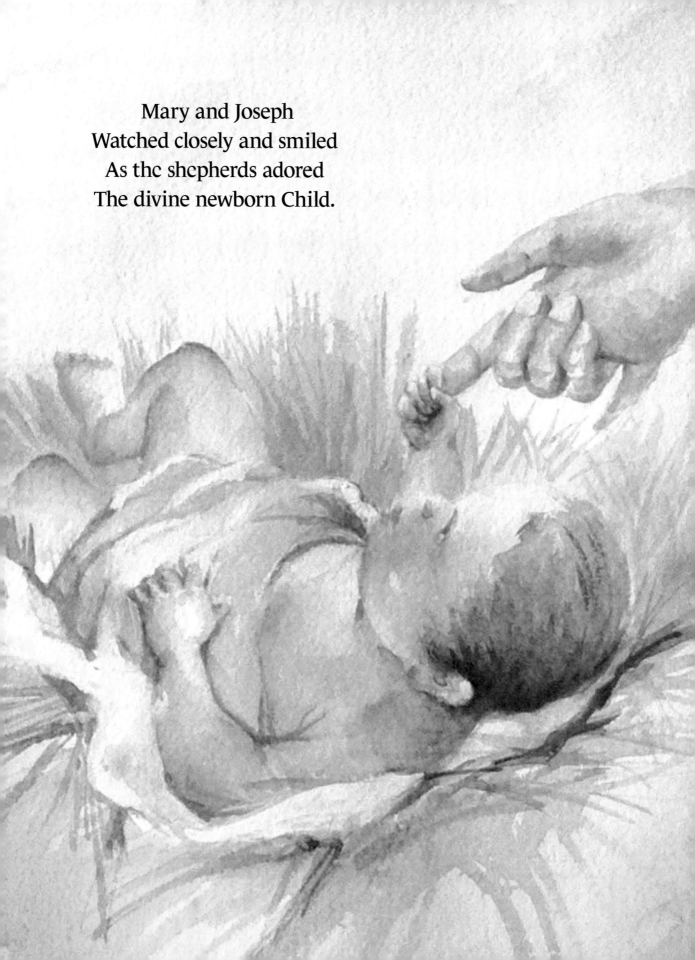

Then David, the oldest,
While the Babe was asleep,
Gave Mary his slingshot
For Jesus to keep.

And Caleb, his brother,
Pulled out his saved treat
And gave Mary the sweet cake
For Jesus to eat.

Then Jacob, their cousin,
Took his cloak in his arms
And gave it to Mary,
To keep Jesus warm.

And Jesse, their neighbor,
Too timid to talk,
Gave Mary his crook
To help Jesus walk.

Then Micah, the youngest,
Looked at Jesus and cried,
"I have nothing to give!"
With his arms open wide.

At the sound of his voice,
Just as soon as he spoke,
The Child in the manger
Softly stirred, then awoke.

Mary's arms, full of gifts,
Had no room for the Child.
She turned then to Joseph,
Who nodded, and smiled,

And picked up the Baby —
The cause of great joy —
And tenderly placed Him
In the arms of the boy.

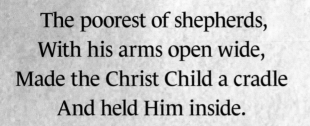

The poorest of shepherds,
With his arms open wide,
Made the Christ Child a cradle
And held Him inside.

The others all watched him,
And smiled when they saw
The dear way he held Jesus,
With wonder and awe.

Now the child who was hungry,
And cold, and so brave,
Held the Baby Who had
A whole world to save.

There in the stable,
In the quiet and still,
The arms that were empty
Were the arms Jesus filled.

And the shepherd who thought
He had nothing to give
Would remember that night
For as long as he lived.

Helping families love and live the Catholic faith

OSV Kids is an exciting new brand on a mission to help children learn about, live, and love the Catholic Faith. Every OSV Kids product is prayerfully developed to introduce children of all ages to Jesus and his Church. Using beautiful artwork, engaging storytelling, and fun activities, OSV Kids products help families form and develop their Catholic identity and learn to live the faith with great joy.

OSV Kids is a monthly magazine that delivers a fun, trustworthy, and faith-filled set of stories, images, and activities designed to help Catholic families with children ages 2-6 build up their domestic churches and live the liturgical year at home.

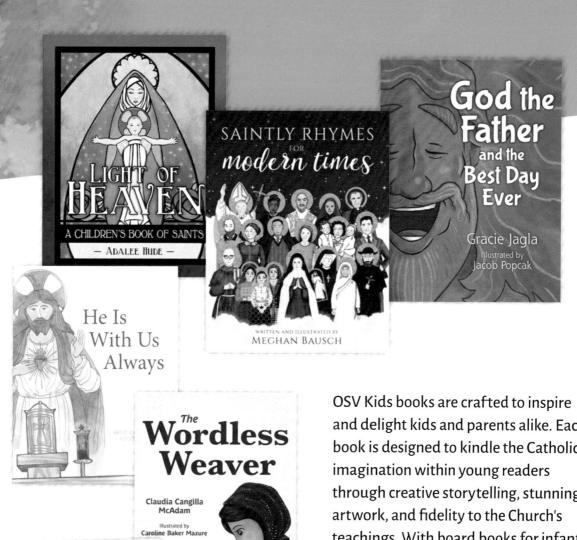

OSV Kids books are crafted to inspire and delight kids and parents alike. Each book is designed to kindle the Catholic imagination within young readers through creative storytelling, stunning artwork, and fidelity to the Church's teachings. With board books for infants and toddlers, picture books for young readers, and exciting stories for older kids, OSV Kids has something for everyone in your family.

Learn more at OSVKids.com

About the Author

Maura Roan McKeegan is the award-winning author of a number of Catholic children's books, including *Into the Sea, Out of the Tomb: Jonah and Jesus*; *St. Conrad and the Wildfire*; and *Where is Jesus Hidden?*. She also writes articles for various magazines. As a former classroom reading teacher, she has a passion for picture books. "I love the way picture books reach across generations to bring the joy and simplicity of childhood to readers of all ages, from the very young to the very old," she says. Reading aloud with children is her favorite hobby.

About the Illustrator

Gina Capaldi has been illustrating children's books for trade and educational publishing houses, and for toy manufacturers, for over twenty-five years. Her historical fiction and nonfiction works have received numerous awards. Gina's new foray into Catholic publishing marks her path of dedication and love of Christ and her faith. When not illustrating, Gina teaches history and art to children at a Southern California Catholic STEM academy.